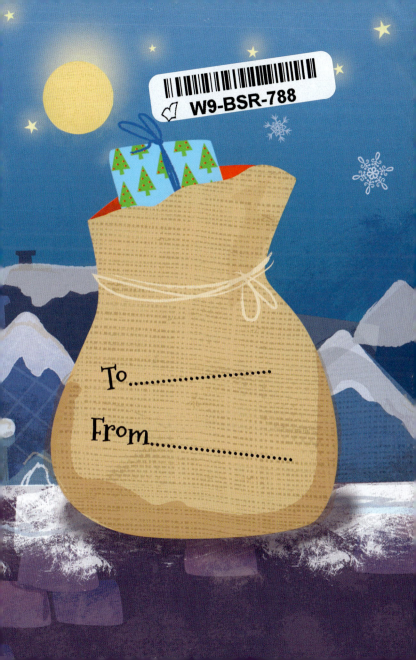

W9-BSR-788

To.....................
From.....................

It was Christmas Eve and I was
snug and warm in my cozy bed.
I was trying so hard to go to sleep.
But I could hear strange noises.

It wasn't the sound of sleigh bells.
It wasn't the sound of reindeer hoofs on the roof.
It wasn't even the sound of Santa unpacking his sack.

It was more of a

HARUMPH!

and an

OOF!

It was no use.

There'd be no sleep for me
until I'd found out what
was making that noise.

I crept down the stairs and peered into the living room. There were three stockings hanging from the fireplace.

One of them belonged to me. But where had the other two come from? Suddenly, a muffled voice came from the chimney.

"Oh, dear. I'm even **more** stuck now!"

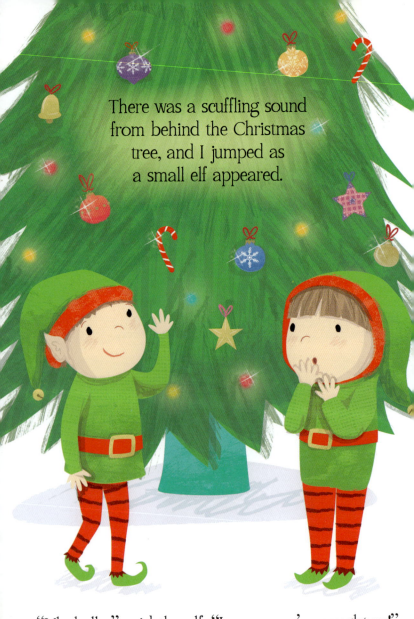

There was a scuffling sound from behind the Christmas tree, and I jumped as a small elf appeared.

"Uh, hello," said the elf. "I guess you've caught us!"

I listened as the elf explained that Santa was stuck in the chimney. The elf had tried to pull him out. But the only things that had come down so far were Santa's boots and pants!

"I can help you," I suggested. "I'll hold Santa's feet and we can both pull." The elf agreed. "Between us, we might be able to get him unstuck."

I grasped both of Santa's feet firmly. But, just at that moment, a light went on upstairs. "Is that you?" called my mom. "Back to bed now, please, or Santa won't come!"

At that exact moment,
Santa shot back up
the chimney... with
me still hanging
onto his feet.

The poor elf could not believe his eyes.
But there was no time to think…
My mom was coming
out of her bedroom.

"Just coming!" squeaked the elf. He hurried
up the stairs and jumped into my bed,
pulling the covers up over his head.
"Night-night, sweetie!" said my
mom through the doorway.

Meanwhile, up on the roof, Santa and I
had landed in a heap. The clever reindeer
had hooked their reins under Santa's arms
and pulled as hard as they could.

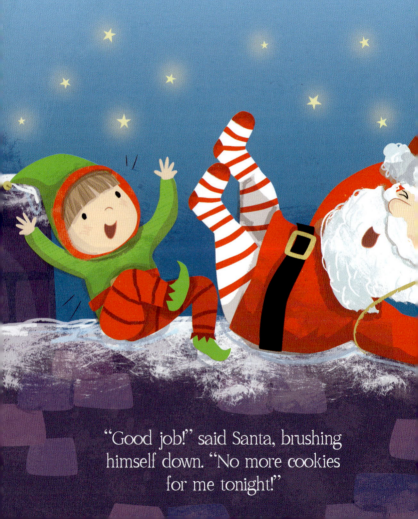

"Good job!" said Santa, brushing
himself down. "No more cookies
for me tonight!"

I scrambled to my feet. But Santa
was so busy, he didn't notice that I
had traded places with the elf!

"I think we'd better deliver the rest of the
presents first," said Santa, "and leave this
house for last."

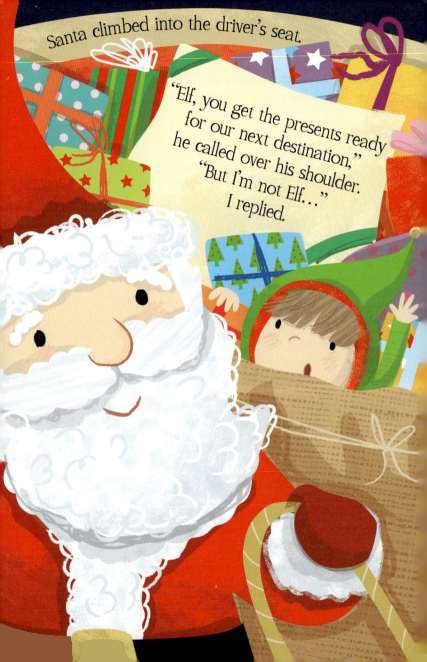

Santa climbed into the driver's seat.

"Elf, you get the presents ready for our next destination," he called over his shoulder.
"But I'm not Elf…" I replied.

Santa wasn't really listening.
He was talking to the reindeer.
"Up, up, and away!" Santa called,
and the reindeer took off
before I had time to explain.

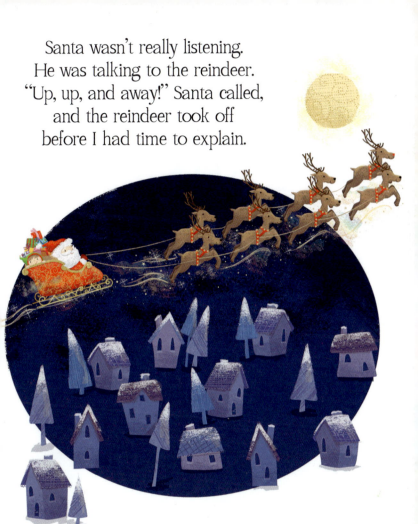

I held on tight as the
sleigh climbed high into the
night sky, above the rooftops.

Surrounded by sacks, I was so busy figuring out which presents were which, there was no time to let Santa know that there'd been a mistake.

There were **big** presents for the cities,

and **SHINY** presents for the towns.

There were **ODD**-shaped presents for the villages,

and **mystery** presents for the farms.

Love from Santa x

As they landed at their next stop, Santa decided that he couldn't risk getting stuck in a chimney again.

"Elf, I think you'd better make the deliveries from now on," decided Santa, "while I sort the presents."

I *shimmied* down chimneys.

I **Squeezed** through cat flaps.

And, if all else failed, I used Santa's *magic* key to let myself in.

In each house, I picked up the cookies to take home to Mrs. Claus, and carrots for the reindeer.

Finally, there was just one sack left, and
Santa still hadn't realized his mistake!
The sleigh headed back over the
rooftops to my house.

Love from
Santa x

I had never had so much fun as when I slid down my own chimney with a sack of my own presents!

I put my presents under the Christmas tree, then picked up Santa's pants and boots and put them in the sack.

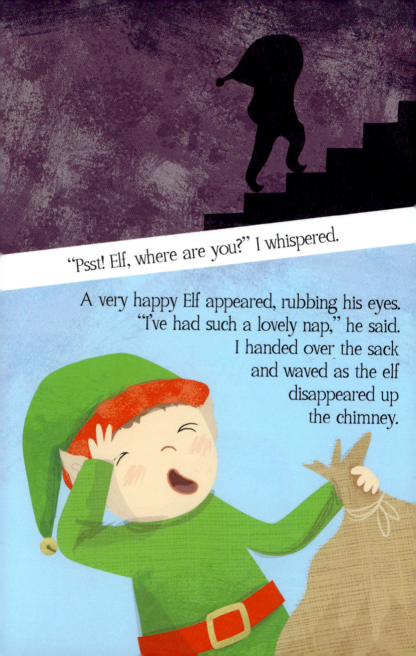

"Psst! Elf, where are you?" I whispered.

A very happy Elf appeared, rubbing his eyes.
"I've had such a lovely nap," he said.
I handed over the sack
and waved as the elf
disappeared up
the chimney.

Back in my cozy bed, I listened to the
sounds of reindeer hoofs on the roof,
sleigh bells, and, very faintly,

"Ho ho ho!

Merry Christmas!"

Or was that,

"Ho ho ho!

yummy cookies!"?

Write your name on the gift tags.

Draw yourself as an elf.

Create one-of-a-kind books for any child on Put Me In The Story!

visit → www.putmeinthestory.com/morenames

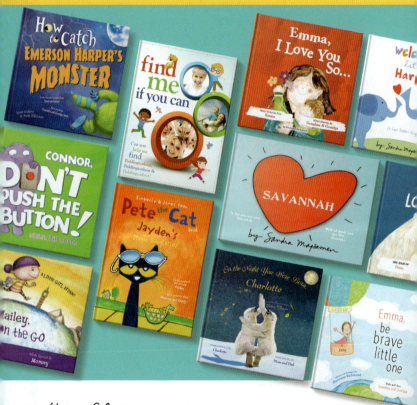

- Find *Unique Gifts* for birthdays, holidays, or any day
- Personalize this and other great stories with *Any Child's Name*
- Choose from over *100 Personalized* versions of bestselling children's books